Published in the United States of America by The Child's World®
1980 Lookout Drive • Mankato, MN 56003-1705
800-599-READ • www.childsworld.com

ACKNOWLEDGMENTS
The Child's World®: Mary Berendes, Publishing Director
The Design Lab: Kathleen Petelinsek, Design and Page Production
Literacy Consultants: Cecilia Minden, PhD, and Joanne Meier, PhD

LIBRARY OF CONGRESS
CATALOGING-IN-PUBLICATION DATA
Moncure, Jane Belk.
  My "r" sound box / by Jane Belk Moncure;
illustrated by Rebecca Thornburgh.
     p. cm. — (Sound box books)
  Summary: "Little r has an adventure with items beginning with
his letter's sound, such as a rooster, a raccoon, and a rowboat
and raft on a rainy river."—Provided by publisher.
  ISBN 978-1-60253-158-1 (library bound : alk. paper)
  [1. Alphabet.] I. Thornburgh, Rebecca McKillip, ill. II. Title.
III. Series.
  PZ7.M739Myr 2009
  [E]—dc22   2008033174

A NOTE TO PARENTS AND EDUCATORS:

Magic moon machines and five fat frogs are just a few of the fun things you can share with children by reading books with them. Reading aloud helps children in so many ways! It introduces them to new words, motivates them to develop their own reading skills, and expands their attention span and listening abilities. So it's important to find time each day to share a book or two . . . or three!

As you read with young children, you can help develop their understanding of how print works by talking about the parts of the book—the cover, the title, the illustrations, and the words that tell the story. As you read, use your finger to point to each word, modeling a gentle sweep from left to right.

Simple word games help develop important prereading skills, including an understanding of rhyme and alliteration (when words share the same beginning sound, such as "six" and "sand"). Try playing with words from a book you've just shared: "What other words start with the same sound as moon?" "Cat and hat, do those words rhyme?" The possibilities are endless—and so are the rewards!

My "r" Sound Box®

WRITTEN BY JANE BELK MONCURE

ILLUSTRATED BY REBECCA THORNBURGH

Little had a box. "I will find things that begin with my **r** sound," he said. "I will put them into my sound box."

Little found rabbits and radishes. Did he put the rabbits and the radishes into the box?

He did.

Little found a rooster. Did he put

the rooster into the box with the

rabbits and the radishes? He did.

Then he found a raccoon. The raccoon ran! Little ran after the raccoon and put it into the box.

Then he saw a rat. The rat ran.

Little ran after the rat and put it into the box. Then he ran down the road.

Soon, Little met a reindeer.

The reindeer 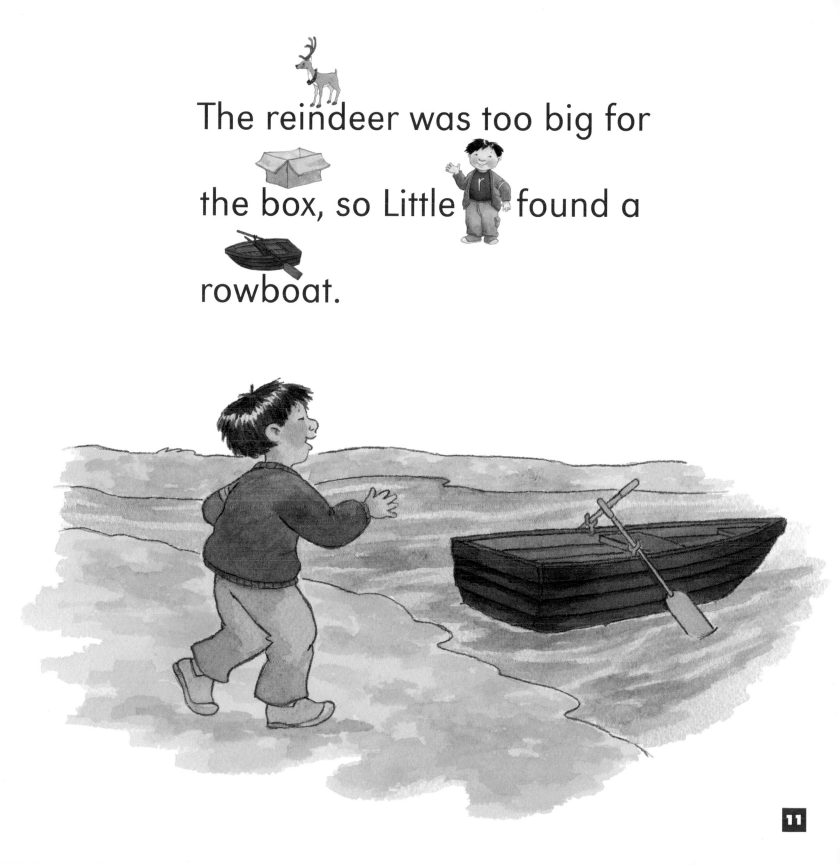 was too big for the box, so Little [boy] found a rowboat.

He put the reindeer and the

box with the rat, the raccoon,

the rooster, and the rabbits

into the rowboat.

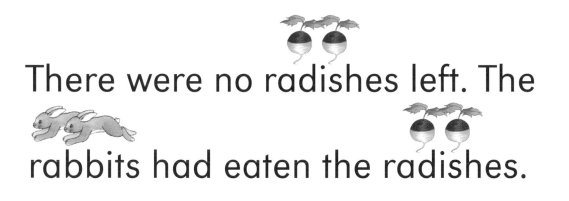

There were no radishes left. The rabbits had eaten the radishes.

Little rowed down the river.

It started to rain. Little put

on his raincoat. He rowed right

into a rhinoceros!

The rhinoceros was too big for the rowboat.

So Little found a raft.

He put all the animals on the raft.

He put the box on the raft, too.

But the raft ran into a rock! The reindeer, the rat, and the rooster fell off the raft.

Little found a rope and

rescued them.

"Now we will rest!" he said.

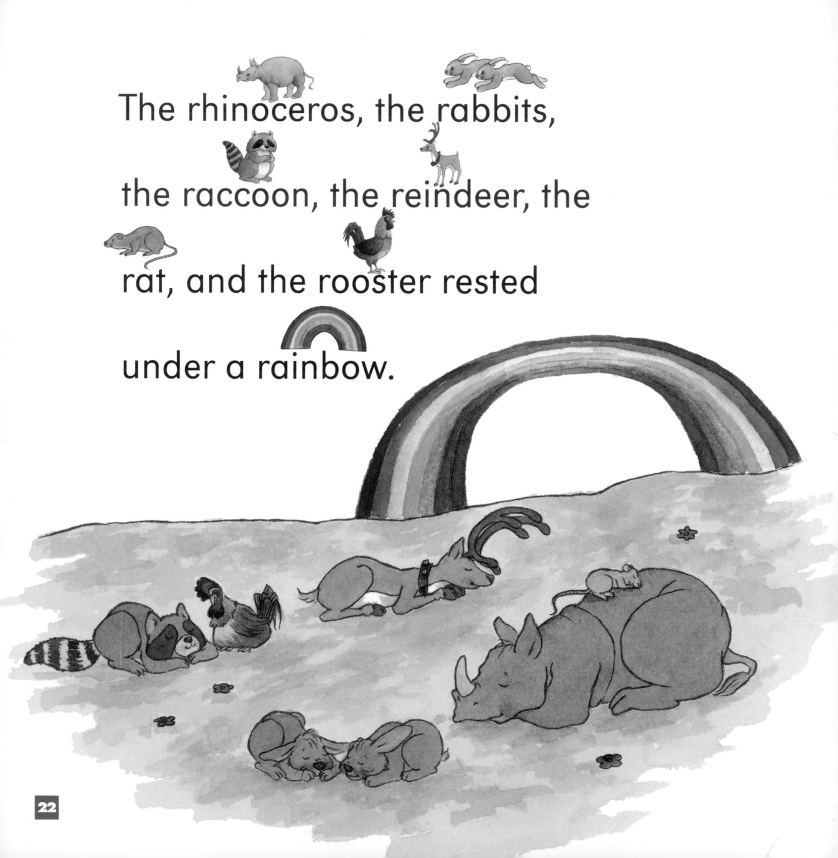

The rhinoceros, the rabbits,

the raccoon, the reindeer, the

rat, and the rooster rested

under a rainbow.

Little rested, too.

Then the rabbits said, "Let's run a race."

They ran up the road to a bush full of roses. Little picked roses for his box.

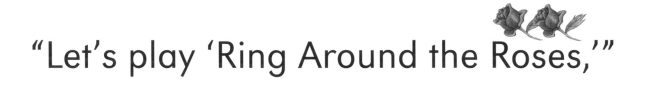

"Let's play 'Ring Around the Roses,'"

he said.

And they did!

Little r's Word List

rabbit

raccoon

race

radish

raft

rain

rainbow

raincoat

rat

reindeer

rhinoceros

river

road

rock

rooster

rope

rose

rowboat

Other Words with Little

radio

raspberry

rattle

razor

rectangle

ribbon

rice

ring

robe

robin

robot

rocket

roof

rug

ruler

More to Do!

Little and his animal friends had a great time playing Ring Around the Roses. Here is another fun rhyming game for you to play!

Directions:

Make up your own verses using the same tune as "Ring Around the Roses." Use as many **r** words as you can think of. You'll also need to think of silly rhyming words. Here are some verses to get you started:

Rhyming:

Ring around the *rabbit*
Pocketful of *babbit*
Silly, silly,
We all fall down!

Ring around the *rocket*
Pocketful of *zocket*
Silly, silly,
We all fall down!

Now you try it!

About the Author

Best-selling author Jane Belk Moncure has written over 300 books throughout her teaching and writing career. After earning a Master's degree in Early Childhood Education from Columbia University, she became one of the pioneers in that field. In 1956, she helped form the Virginia Association for Early Childhood Education, which established the first statewide standards for teachers of young children.

Inspired by her work in the classroom, Mrs. Moncure's books have become standards in primary education, and her name is recognized across the country. Her success is reflected not only in her books' popularity with parents, children, and educators, but also by numerous awards, including the 1984 C. S. Lewis Gold Medal Award.

About the Illustrator

Rebecca Thornburgh lives in a pleasantly spooky old house in Philadelphia. If she's not at her drawing table, she's reading—or singing with her band, called Reckless Amateurs. Rebecca has one husband, two daughters, and two silly dogs.